Little Book of Lists

GUS SILBER is a freelance magazine journalist, scriptwriter, and author of five books, including *It Takes Two to Toyi-Toyi, Braaivleis of the Vanities,* and *Gus Silber's Little Book of Lists* (that's the one you're reading now).

ANTHONY STIDOLPH, of Pietermaritzburg, is a former civil servant and turkey-plucker who dropped out to become a cartoonist. He draws the pictures in the *Natal Witness,* and has collaborated with Gus Silber on several books. Stidolph's ambition is to be a Viking.

Gus Silber's Little Book of Lists

with illustrations
by Anthony Stidolph

PENGUIN BOOKS

PENGUIN BOOKS

Published by the Penguin Group
27 Wrights Lane, London W8 5TZ, England
Viking Penguin, a division of Penguin Books USA Inc,
375 Hudson Street, New York, New York 10014, USA
Penguin Books Australia Ltd, Ringwood, Victoria, Australia
Penguin Books Canada Ltd, 10 Alcorn Avenue,
Toronto, Ontario, Canada M4V 3B2
Penguin Books (NZ) Ltd, 182-190 Wairau Road,
Auckland 10, New Zealand
Penguin Books, Amethyst Street, Theta Ext 1,
Johannesburg, South Africa

Penguin Books Ltd, Registered Offices:
Harmondsworth, Middlesex, England

First published by Penguin Books 1995

ISBN 0 140 25649 0

Typeset by Positive Proof cc
Printed and bound by The Rustica Press (Pty) Ltd, Old Mill Road, Ndabeni
Cover design by Hadaway Illustration & Design

D4360

CONTENTS

TOP TEN LEAST LIKELY NEW PUBLIC HOLIDAYS

1. National Women Drivers' Day
2. National Party Day
3. National Panasonic Day
4. National Volkstaat Boundary Declaration Day
5. National Early Tax Return Day
6. National 'It's a Man's, Man's, Man's, Man's World' Day
7. National Former Security Policemen Confession Day
8. National 'Victory in '96 Olympics' Day
9. National Commemoration of FW de Klerk's Big Speech Day
10. National Maid's Day Off

TOP TEN TRAFFIC SAFETY TIPS FOR CELLULAR PHONE USERS

1. Use both elbows to steer while dialling number
2. Form orderly queue to dial '112' at scene of roadside emergency
3. To avoid permanent hearing damage, change ears at least every 15 to 20 kilometres
4. If battery runs out in middle of important call, make sure window is open before hurling phone into path of oncoming traffic
5. Try to keep at least one hand on wheel while having argument with spouse
6. Turn off car-radio when participating in a Talkback show, as feedback interferes with reception
7. It is illegal to use your cellphone to warn other road-users of speed traps, unless you are calling to tell them to stop flashing their brights at you
8. If phone rings as you pull away from a traffic light, remember to change to second gear at some stage on your journey

9. If phone doesn't ring at all during your journey, stop staring at it

10. Install hands-free cellular phone car-kit for optimum safety, but bear in mind that other road-users will no longer be able to tell that you are on your cell

'Hello, 112? I'd like to report a small roadside emergency.'

TOP TEN DEMANDS OF THE SPRINGBOK RUGBY SQUAD

1. Fifteen per cent royalty on all public performances of 'Shosholoza'
2. Guaranteed listing on JSE for any player scoring more than two tries in an international test match
3. 'Stunt Squad' to be formed to play matches in inclement weather conditions
4. Springbok symbol to be replaced on rotating basis by logo of highest-bidding corporate sponsor
5. Half-time naartjies to be replaced by Big Mac, Fries, and Shake
6. Autographing of balls and programmes to be sub-contracted to outside Public Relations team
7. All refereeing decisions and lineout calls to be channelled through players' attorneys
8. 'One Team, One Nation' to be registered as trademark for exclusive use on authorised merchandise

9. Players entitled to two practice nights off a week to accommodate busy 'personal appearance' schedule

10. No extra time without extra pay

On-field legal representation – one of the top ten demands of the Springbok rugby squad

TOP TEN REASONS WINNIE MANDELA COULDN'T MAKE IT TO OPENING OF PARLIAMENT

1. Having a 'bad hat' day
2. Thought big red circle on calendar meant 'Stayaway'
3. Couldn't decide which necklace to wear
4. Didn't want to miss live coverage of Opening of Parliament on television
5. Busy practising sullen expression in mirror, didn't realise what time it was
6. Hair-bead got caught in door on way out
7. Decided to collect salary on day after opening, when it's a little quieter
8. Against interim constitution to fire a person more than twice
9. Wanted to finish cleaning house in case of police raid
10. New maid put camouflage uniform on hot cycle, shrank two sizes

TOP TEN REASONS WHY BLOEMFONTEIN SHOULD BE SOUTH AFRICA'S NEW PARLIAMENTARY CAPITAL

1. No traffic noise to awaken Parliamentarians during speeches by Mangosuthu Buthelezi

2. Some of the country's top safari-suit tailors within easy walking distance of Parliament

3. Free Volkspele performances in promenade during recess

4. No foreign tourists nagging for autographs outside Parliament

5. City boasts attractive fountain made entirely from flowers

6. You can park your car with the doors unlocked and the engine running, and no one will be able to work out how to steal it

7. Permits no longer required for overnight stays by English-speaking South Africans

8. City offers excellent opportunities for economic growth and industrial development, if only because there isn't any at the moment

9. Only place in the country where they still know how to mix a decent Cane & Coke

10. Tranquil atmosphere is conducive to the passing of firm resolutions on postponement of legislation

EUGENE TERRE'BLANCHE'S TOP TEN PLANS FOR BOOSTING AWB MEMBERSHIP

1. Members of other race groups now welcome to join elite 'Washing & Ironing' unit

2. Uniforms now available in three shades of Khaki: 'Castle Lager Khaki', 'Klipdrif Khaki', and 'Khaki En Betaal'

3. New 'short-sleeve' policy gives all AWB members the right to bare arms

4. Membership fee now structured on sliding scale, with contributions declining in inverse proportion to size of paunch

5. Every stormtrooper gets a free umbrella to use in inclement weather

6. New members qualify for discounted premiums on horseriding insurance

7. Meetings specially arranged to avoid clashes with 'The Bold & the Beautiful' on CCV

8. New members stand in line to win season ticket to protest international rugby test matches at Loftus Versveld

9. Free tie with AWB insignia for court appearances

10. Special daytrip to Sun City once a month to scout locations for new Volkstaat

TOP TEN NEW PROGRAMMES SCHEDULED FOR RADIO SAFM

1. 'The Govan Reddy Hour'. Spend five minutes in the company of the pleasant, urbane head of South Africa's favourite FM radio station
2. 'Commercial Break'. Tune in to SAfm at any time of day for a refreshing break from irritating commercials
3. 'Microphone Not In'. Hundreds of listeners call in to say they can't hear a word Nigel Murphy is saying because his microphone is not plugged in, and would he please leave it that way
4. 'The Pot & Kettle Show'. Live coverage of SAfm's early morning editorial conference, featuring reaction by management and staff to 702's plunging listenership figures
5. 'The Daily Serial Murderer'. Panic and mystery at a top regional radio station, as someone decides to drop the daily Agatha Christie serial in favour of a new series on Ndebele interior decorating

The launch of South Africa's favourite FM radio station

6. 'Accents on South Africa'. A regular spotlight on the rich diversity of accents employed by South Africans calling in to complain about the accents on SAfm
7. 'Letter From London'. An expatriate South African talks about the pleasures of life in England, where you can't get SAfm
8. 'Novel Reading'. A popular SAfm announcer reads the new blockbuster novel by John Grisham instead of coming to work, and nobody notices
9. 'Daily Meditation'. A few minutes of soothing, soulful contemplation at the end of another hard working day on SAfm
10. 'Daily Mediation'. An industrial relations negotiating team is called in to persuade late-night studio staff to wake up and go back to work in case someone out there is listening

Some of the top ten words you can make from '!Khoisan X'

TOP TEN WORDS YOU CAN MAKE FROM '!KHOISAN X'

1. Nix! (Short form of name of former American President, used to save space in headlines)
2. Koi! (Type of expensive goldfish)
3. Shank! (Part of an ox)
4. Ox! (Where shanks come from)
5. Sonix! (Name of minor-league softball team from Pittsburgh)
6. Oasix! (More than one oasis)
7. Inoxa! (Type of facial lotion)
8. Sani-X! (New Extra-Strong household disinfectant)
9. Honki! (Derogatory form of 'Settler')
10. Six! (Number of votes PAC got in last election)

ALFRED NZO'S TOP TEN FOREIGN POLICY DECISIONS

1. Decided to buy one of those desktop globes of the world that light up as you spin them around
2. Decided to order Chinese takeaway instead of Italian for lunch at the office
3. Decided to call Pik Botha to remind him to send someone around to collect empties from cabinet
4. Decided to adopt diplomatic policy of 'Two Chinas', and invite both of them round for a braai at his house on Sunday
5. Decided to make important public statement on South Africa's foreign policy towards Bosnia-Herzegovina
6. Decided against it
7. Decided to appear on Agenda-Newsline to refute allegations that South Africa does not have a foreign policy to speak of
8. Decided to request SABC Board to take stern disciplinary action against security guard who refused

to let him into building on grounds of never having heard of him

9. Decided to call Pik Botha again to ask him where exactly you have to tear the paper to make a rudder on those little Origami aeroplanes

10. Decided against involving Foreign Affairs Department in Nigerian human rights crisis, on grounds that countries in Africa cannot really be regarded as 'foreign'

Alfred Nzo deciding whether or not to make a Foreign Policy decision

GILL MARCUS'S TOP TEN FASHION TIPS

1. Keep kaftans and bedspreads in separate cupboards to avoid confusion
2. In cold weather, wear jersey underneath kaftan, otherwise people might think you are wearing a skirt
3. To avoid embarrassment, never wear a kaftan in colours of South African flag to any event where a choir is scheduled to perform
4. Never attempt to cross a road at a pedestrian crossing while wearing a kaftan with black and white stripes
5. Always ensure kaftan is completely inside car before closing door
6. For opening of Parliament and other formal occasions, avoid wearing kaftans in same design as President's shirt
7. Satin kaftans are powerful conductors of static electricity, so always wear rubber-soled shoes when shaking hands with anyone who is not a member of the National Party

8. Predictions for this season: hemlines down, necklines up, sleevelines to stay the same

9. Pockets sewn inside kaftan come in handy at cocktail parties and other buffet functions

10. For added safety, sew ball-bearings in hemline of kaftan during south-easter season in Cape Town

A Gill Marcus fashion tip

TOP TEN CONFESSIONS OF 'SUPERSPY' CRAIG WILLIAMSON

1. Once mistakenly ordered his Martini stirred instead of shaken
2. Frequently used to listen to Country & Western music on his wristwatch radio transmitter
3. Placed hundreds of bugs in the Entomology Department at Wits University without being discovered
4. As result of mix-up of orders, once poured tank of petrol into left-wing activist's sugar-bowl
5. Came close to blowing cover by trying to infiltrate leftwing splinter branch of Anorexics Anonymous
6. Sparked major scandal at Wits University by revealing that an outspoken leftwing activist on campus was not a Police spy
7. Was in line for promotion to 'Super-duper-spy' until cover was officially lifted
8. Once came very close to blowing cover by being able to sing more than three words of 'Nkosi Sikelel'

iAfrika' during rally at Wits in the Seventies

9. Out of force of habit, still eats all faxes marked 'Private & Confidential' after reading

10. Welcomes opportunity to testify before Truth and Reconciliation Commission, as long as he is allowed to give evidence in his native Russian

How not to commit a 'dirty trick'

TOP TEN WAYS TO FOIL CAR HIJACKERS

1. Treat all robots and four-way stop streets as yield signs
2. Don't yield
3. Paint 'Help! My car has just been hijacked ' in large letters on roof of car
4. Do not open window more than 1mm to accept pamphlets on anti-hijacking security systems
5. Put loudspeaker on roof, and urge people to register to vote in Local Government elections
6. Hoot loudly, flash lights, and drive in an aggressive, threatening manner to avoid attracting attention on the road
7. Put fake satellite dish on roof for 24-hour fake satellite surveillance
8. If driving minibus, do not stop to pick up persons with thumb in air and index finger in horizontal position; means 'I have a gun'
9. Paint car canary-yellow, wear dark-blue clothes, and drive like a lunatic

10. Buy a Toyota Corolla – keeps going right, so hijackers will only be able to drive in a circle

Warning: This man has just signalled his intention to hijack your vehicle

Cutting down on harmful second helpings,
the Louis Luyt way

LOUIS LUYT'S TOP TEN DIET TIPS

1. Never shout at people with your mouth full
2. Resist picking at food left on table by people who have stormed out of room during your post-match victory speech
3. Cut down on harmful second helpings by ordering bigger first helpings
4. Reduce syrup intake by unplaiting koeksisters before eating
5. Put picture of Louis Luyt on fridge door
6. Refrain from eating after-dinner mints until after dinner
7. Buy suits two sizes too big – pulling up trousers in public conveys positive impression of weight reduction efforts
8. Never eat on an empty stomach
9. Try not to overindulge at post-match functions, unless Springboks have won or lost
10. Make every possible effort to eliminate humble pie from your diet

TOP TEN REASONS WHY THE 2004 OLYMPICS SHOULD BE HELD IN BEIJING

1. No big mountain to interfere with global satellite reception
2. No sunswept, golden beaches to distract visitors from Olympic events
3. No giant Pick 'n Pay hoardings to obscure view at stadium
4. Fewer tourists from Gauteng
5. Fewer Capetonians
6. Prospect of exciting 'tank-assisted' sprint events in Tiananmen Square
7. Presence of international media will force Beijing authorities to cut down on public executions of pickpockets and traffic offenders
8. On the other hand, there could be a dramatic increase in public executions of Chinese long-distance athletes who finish second
9. Less chance of post-games address by 'tired and emotional' Louis Luyt
10. KWV export wine available in Chinese restaurants in Beijing

Tank-assisted sprint event,
Beijing Olympics, 2004

TOP TEN PUBLIC CONCERNS ABOUT THE RISING TIDE OF PORNOGRAPHY IN SOUTH AFRICA

1. Rash of sleazy titles on open display at corner cafés makes it increasingly difficult for decent, law-abiding citizens to decide which one to buy

2. Promised eau de cologne samples are often missing from 'Paco Rabane' ads in Playboy

3. Innocent bystanders are routinely elbowed in stomach by people carelessly ripping open plastic shrinkwrap

4. Studies in America show that hardcore pornography is a contributing factor in nine out of ten postgraduate research projects by Sociology students

5. Publishers of pornography claim a Constitutional right to 'free expression', yet their magazines sell for up to R15 a copy

6. Pornography is widely available on the 'Internet' – but what about the millions of bona fide anti-

pornography researchers who do not have access to computers?

7. Brisk turning of pages by bona fide anti-pornography researchers can lead to painful 'paper cuts' on fingers

Getting pornography out of South Africa's bookshops – a tall order

8. By putting porno mags out of reach on top shelf, bookstores could be contravening 'Short Persons' amendment to Bill of Rights
9. Every time you open one of those magazines, all sorts of little inserts and subscription cards come tumbling out
10. Even if safeguarded from pornography by responsible adults, minors can still inadvertently encounter it by switching on Agenda-Newsline when Horace van Rensburg is in the studio

TOP TEN REASONS WHY ALLAN BOESAK IS INNOCENT

1. Proven commitment to fighting poverty in Allan Boesak household

2. Made positive contribution to Reconstruction and Development Programme by extending kitchen and installing second jacuzzi in Cape Town mansion

3. He and Elna Boesak are just good friends

4. Strongly believes South Africa's legacy of social problems will not be surmounted by handing millions of Rand in foreign aid money to the homeless

5. Voluntarily resigned from position as Ambassador-designate to Geneva when integrity was under attack

6. Only opened private bank account in Geneva in case resignation was turned down

7. Those black, bloodstained gloves are way too small for his hands

8. Whoops – wrong case

9. Can prove he was out of the country when those large amounts were mysteriously deposited into his private bank account

10. Had to receive medical attention when fingers were caught in till

WINNIE MANDELA'S TOP TEN ANSWERING-MACHINE MESSAGES

1. Hello. This is Winnie Mandela. I'm not in right now, but if you'd like to leave a summons, please put it in the big black bag next to the security gate
2. Hello. You've reached the residence of Winnie Mandela. No one is available to take your call right now, but if you'd like to hold on for a few minutes, you may leave a message with the senior policeman in charge of the raid
3. Hello. This is Winnie Mandela, Deputy Minister of Science, Arts, and Technology, and this is a very old message
4. Hello. This is Winnie Mandela. I've gone out to buy a hat. Please try again in a few weeks' time
5. Hello. This is Winnie Mandela. I'm not in at the moment, but if you'd like to make a donation to the Committee to Assist the Suffering and Homeless, please make your cheque out to CASH
6. Hello. You've reached the office of Winnie Mandela. I'm not available

right now, because Parliament is in session. So please try me on my cellphone at the Hyde Park Corner shopping centre

7. Hello. You've reached the office of Winnie Mandela. Dial 1 to hear my views on the liberation of women from the yoke of male tyranny. Dial 2 to hear what I have to say about the inherent ineffectiveness of the Truth and Reconciliation Commission. Dial 3. . .
8. Hello. You've reached the private, unlisted line of Winnie Mandela. Please leave a message stating name, telephone number, circulation of magazine, and angle of intended interview
9. Hi! Thanks for calling! Hope you're having a lovely day! I'd really love to come to the phone and chat with you, but I'm afraid I can't, because you've just dialled the wrong number!
10. The number you have dialled is unavailable. Please try again when the telephone has been reconnected. For further information, contact the Accounts Department of your nearest Telkom office

TOP TEN TIPPING GUIDELINES FOR FIRST-TIME FOREIGN VISITORS TO JOHANNESBURG

1. Airport Baggage Handler: between R5 and R10, to be paid directly to airport security officer who catches person in act of handling your baggage
2. Minibus Taxi Driver: between 10 and 15 per cent of fare for driver, and 25 to 30 per cent for rear-gunner on roof-rack
3. Freelance Parking Attendant: between 10 and 15 per cent of the insurance excess on your panel-beating bill
4. Informal Street Trader: minimum of 10 per cent of high-denomination note handed over for change for parking meter, rising to 25 per cent if traffic warden is less than two blocks away
5. Boerewors Roll Vendor: discretionary, based on overall length of boerewors in relation to roll, and amount of mustard applied before enquiring whether you would like mustard with your roll

6. Plainclothes Police Inner-City Shopping Escort: in terms of new code of ethics, no member of the force may accept any gratuity over and above the standard ten per cent commission paid by shopholders for directing tourists into their shops

When travelling by minibus taxi, don't forget to tip the roof-rack rear-gunner

7. Hotel Chambermaid: up to R5 per day, payable at end of stay, with further professional fee to be negotiated if chambermaid is quizzed on sociopolitical viewpoints and developments by journalist working on rush story on new South African society

8. Telkom Repair Person: Telkom regulations strictly forbid personnel from accepting gratuities for professional services rendered, so feel free to tip at your own discretion

9. Petrol Pump Attendant: up to R5 for exceptionally friendly and caring super-service, or a fixed R7.50 for just sticking in the petrol and getting on with it

10. Inner-City Tour Guide: minimum of R2.50 per hour of touring city's side-streets and back-alleys by foot, or a flat R25 for conducting the tour by car on the way to Sandton City

TOP TEN THINGS DAVID HALL-GREEN COULD DO TO LIVEN UP 'GOOD MORNING SOUTH AFRICA'

1. Cartwheel on to set wearing candy-striped hipster trousers and 'Bozo the Clown' wig
2. Announce that Martians have landed in Vanderbijlpark, and would everyone please evacuate their homes
3. Make crude off-camera remark about incompetence of SABC sound technicians
4. Pretend not to notice that he has come to work without any clothes on, and this time it isn't a dream
5. Offer R500 000 cash reward to first caller who can prove he has been watching three-way live panel discussion on Government's draft White Paper on land redistribution
6. Take R50 bill out of wallet, roll up tightly, and casually insert in left nostril during four-way live panel discussion on 'National Substance Abuse Week'
7. Interrupt interview with famed international arteriosclerosis expert

to order toasted bacon-and-egg sandwich from SABC canteen

8. Say 'And now it's over to Alyce Chavunduka for the seven o'clock News. Yo, Alyce! What's happening, babe?'

9. During early-morning anecdote-swapping session, tell Dorianne Berry there's a big spider in her hair

10. Get another job

The search for intelligent life on Good Morning South Africa

A truthful and reconciliatory person testifies before the Truth and Reconciliation Commission

TOP TEN THINGS NOT TO TELL THE TRUTH AND RECONCILIATION COMMISSION

1. Can we hurry this up? I'm double-parked outside
2. If this is about that overdue library book, I can explain everything
3. I was only issuing orders
4. You've got the wrong guy. I was in Bolivia from 1976 to 1989
5. If you don't mind, I'd like to keep my sunglasses on while I testify
6. I'd like to consult with my literary agent before I answer that question
7. You can't prove a thing!
8. Does the name 'McCarthy' mean anything to you?
9. If you want to know the truth, I don't believe in reconciliation
10. Ha! Only joking, Your Honour

TOP TEN WAYS TO SAVE WATER FOR A RAINY DAY

1. Buy portable water tanker, and follow Fire Brigade to scene of major emergencies
2. Adjust shower to 'scalding' before entering cubicle
3. Raise the level of your swimming-pool by throwing a few rocks in the deep end
4. For a healthy, refreshing beverage, try undiluted orange concentrate
5. Swap dog for camel
6. Water garden using 'drip irrigation' method
7. Fix drip
8. For a change, take tea with milk and no water
9. Cars that have not been washed for several weeks are easier to track down when hijacked
10. To locate underground water in your garden, dowse with forked stick, and dig until you strike municipal water main

'Excuse me, would you mind saving some of that water for me ...'

TOP TEN NEW PUBLIC SERVICE CHANNELS PLANNED BY THE SABC

1. The Autocue Channel. Instead of watching newsreaders and Agenda-Newsline presenters battling to see what's on the autocue, switch to this channel and read the autocue for yourself. You're bound to do a better job

2. The Tunnel Channel. Live, 24-hour coverage from the inside of the Channel Tunnel, which at least has a little light at the end of it

3. The Election Channel. A special information and education channel devoted entirely to in-depth documentaries, features, debates and talkshows on 'How the SABC is going to be covering the forthcoming election'

4. The Public Service Channel. As a public service, the SABC advises viewers of the exciting range of new releases now available at your neighbourhood video store

5. The Public Servants' Channel. On air from 8am to 8.30am, 9am to 9.30am, 11am to 11.15am, 12pm to 12.20pm, and 2.45pm to 4pm Monday to Friday, this action-packed channel will give public servants around the country something to watch during working hours

6. The Reconstruction and Development Channel. Tune in for live, round-the-clock coverage of the SABC's new 'We Have A Problem, Please Be Patient' logo

7. The Afrikaans Channel. Following a storm of protest by Afrikaans television viewers, the SABC proves its commitment to minority-language broadcasting with a special channel devoted to Afrikaans culture, history, and tradition. From 9am to 9.03am daily

8. The Channel Islands Channel. Not many people know where the Channel Islands are, or why so many of them are named after cows. Charl Pauw investigates

9. The Official Channel. An official channel for the airing of grievances by SABC employees, to prevent

them from bombarding the print media with allegations that the SABC never takes any notice of grievances aired through official channels

10. The Channel of Champions. Sorry, that's M-Net

TOP TEN INCOME-GENERATING OPPORTUNITIES FOR SMALL BUSINESS ENTREPRENEURS

1. Cell-U-Rent: Roadside cellular phone rental service for motor vehicle hijackees
2. Boards-'R-Us: All-weather cardboard signs designed and hand-lettered to your specifications for use at major traffic intersections throughout the country
3. Hub-U-Eat: Impress your dinner guests with hand-beaten dinner plates made entirely from BMW hubcaps
4. Park-Your-Self: For a small fee, our specially trained freelance parking attendants will move out of the way and desist from making gratuitous hand signals in your rearview mirror while you attempt to park your car in central Johannesburg
5. LorryBack Sales and Distribution: All prices smashed on wide range of china crockery, farm-fresh eggs, and cut-glass crystal champagne goblets that fell off the back of a lorry

Freelance Foreign Exchange Dealer – one of the top ten South African entrepreneurship opportunities

6. Porn-2-Go: Rid our country's retail outlets of the scourge of pornography by ordering books, magazines, videotapes and other items to go
7. RDP Novelties: Unique memento for foreign visitors – get the full list of successful Government Reconstruction and Development projects inscribed on a single grain of rice by our expert Chinese calligraphers
8. Bulk Paper Recycling: Make big bucks and help conserve the environment by pulping press releases, speeches, and draft Constitutional submissions issued by the Minister of Home Affairs
9. Foreign Exchange Dealer: Trade Dollars, Sterling, Yen, and Deutschmark for your life on any street corner in Hillbrow
10. House-Sitting: Look after luxury suburban properties while owners are away on holiday, and ignore Court Order to move out when they return

KOBUS WIESE'S TOP TEN THINGS TO DO DURING A 30-DAY SUSPENSION

1. Unravel insulation tape and check whether ears are still in place
2. Learn how to sign autograph without smearing ink all over rugby ball
3. Take up squash and apply for position in National Squad to play Wales
4. Learn fourth word to 'Nkosi Sikelel' iAfrika'
5. Try to work out how to remove bicycle shorts without first removing rugby shorts
6. Try to change lightbulb using 'lineout jump' technique
7. Find out which automatic washing-powder works best at removing stubborn stains from Springbok rugby jersey
8. Buy a pair of dark glasses and carry on playing for Springbok Squad
9. Ask Louis Luyt for a raise
10. Count to 30

Exclusive: Kobus Wiese untaping his ears during a 30-day suspension

TOP TEN SECOND LINES TO 'SHOSHOLOZA', AS SUNG BY NINE OUT OF TEN WHITE SOUTH AFRICANS

1. Yebo Gogo
2. Hamba Kahle
3. Sikelele
4. Mama Thembu
5. Dan Moyane
6. Amaboko
7. Shosholoza (repeat)
8. Amandla Awethu
9. Stimela-a-a-a, Stimela
10. Haya! Haya! Haya Ipi Tombi-yum

'Shosholoza! Er, that's it ...'

TOP TEN PERKS OF BEING A MEMBER OF PARLIAMENT

1. Exclusive membership of 'Frequent Free Flyer' club on South African Airways
2. VIP seating at Newlands Rugby Ground when Parliament is in session, including direct satellite link to let you know how Budget Vote is going
3. Free television licence gives you licence to say anything you want to on television
4. No tax payable on income earned from sub-letting holiday cottage in Hermanus when Parliament is in recess
5. Choice of up to three meat dishes with your gravy when you travel to work on the Blue Train
6. Annual all-expenses-paid trip to Bahamas, with spouse and family, to attend international conference on Third World debt repayment crisis
7. Complimentary closed-circuit video system installed at your official residence, to let you know when the Sheriff is coming

8. 'MP On Duty' windshield sticker entitles bearer to free all-day parking outside any casino resort in southern Africa

9. Extra cheese on your pizza when you order a takeaway from any participating Pizza Hut

10. Work Flexi-Time, get paid for Maxi-Time

A Sheriff arrives at the official residence of an Honourable Member of Parliament

TOP TEN ANTI-THEFT DEVICES FOR YOUR CAR

1. Gorilla Lock (Lock gorilla in car while you do your shopping)
2. Silent Alarm (Insistent, piercing alarm suddenly goes silent when car is broken into, alerting all in vicinity that something is drastically wrong)
3. Rent-a-Dent (Authentic-looking painted dents make your car less desirable to thieves, who will leave it alone after adding a few dents of their own)
4. BackSeat Driver (Forced entry activates recorded voice of nagging spouse, forcing thieves to abandon car and take bus instead)
5. BackSeat Talkshow Host (Cardboard cut-out of Felicia Mabuza-Suttle, complete with clipboard and list of ready-to-ask questions for special edition on crime in South Africa)
6. 'How Am I Driving' Sticker (Motorist with cellphone calls number and gives point-by-point

commentary to policeman who answers phone, allowing instant comparison with computerised read-out of legitimate owner's driving habits)

7. Flag-'em-Down (If car is operated without secret code, six-colour inkjets will spray from centre of steering-wheel on to face of driver, facilitating identification outside of major international sporting events)

'Gorilla Lock' security device in action

8. Auto-Shocker (As thief attempts to gain entry, he will be shocked off his feet by recorded voice revealing how much it costs to install an effective security system in your car these days)

9. Eject-A-Seat (Wing-Mirror-mounted remote video camera relays pictures to base station, where response officer can press button to eject unauthorised driver as car rounds Chapman's Peak)

10. Car-Jack (Make life difficult for thieves by removing left rear wheel and leaving car standing on jack whenever you have to park it in town for a few minutes)

TOP TEN DEFINITIONS OF CURRENT SOUTH AFRICAN POLITICAL TERMS

1. Transparency: Policy of encouraging openness and clarity in public administration, by distributing envelopes with clear plastic windows to select Government officials
2. Accountability: Ability of top Government officials to open bank accounts in Switzerland
3. Truth and Reconciliation: Art of balancing income and expenditure while filling out tax return
4. Reconstruction and Development: Business as usual during extensions to Sandton City shopping complex
5. Economic Empowerment: Full turn-out of Members of Parliament for Budget Vote on Parliamentary salary increases
6. Inclusiveness: Taking your spouse and children with you on Government fact-finding missions to foreign countries
7. Consultation: Service rendered for less than R15 000 a day by consultant hired to investigate

overspending by Government departments

8. Gender Equality: Why women are just as capable as men of heading an organisation like the ANC Women's League

9. Non Government Organisation: South African Government

10. Affirmative Action: Switching off TV1 at 8pm and going out to hire a video

TOP TEN SIGNS THAT YOUR BANK COULD BE HEADING FOR A CRASH

1. Strict limit of R50 per day imposed on cash withdrawals by auto-teller muggers
2. Bank manager calls you up and asks for a loan to tide him over until payday
3. Bank offers free 'ballpoint-pen-on-chain' to all clients making cash deposits of R50 000 or more
4. Bank announces attractive new 'indefinite fixed deposit' savings scheme, paying dividends of up to ten cents in the Rand to successful creditors
5. Bank promotes environmental awareness by asking clients to return 'Refer to Drawer' cheques for recycling
6. Bank imposes mandatory five-year clearance period on salary cheques
7. Bank exchanges safe for refrigerator in preparation for freezing of deposits
8. Staff members wear full-face motorcycle crash helmets to work

9. Directors of bank issue Press Statement denouncing media speculation and assuring investors that their capital is safe and sound

10. Directors of bank fly to Zurich to double-check that their capital is safe and sound

TOP TEN SIGNS THAT YOUR NEIGHBOUR MAY BE AN ILLEGAL ALIEN

1. Asks if he can borrow your satellite dish to phone home
2. Tries to conduct a conversation with your cat
3. Watches SABC News, and seems to understand what Jay Naidoo is talking about
4. Invites you over for a braai, and ignites firelighters just by looking at them
5. Falls on floor laughing when he sees your brand-new, state-of-the-art Pentium computer
6. Joins you for a night out at a restaurant, and boldly goes where no man has gone before – into the ladies' cloakroom
7. Admits he didn't know South Africa won World Rugby Cup
8. Asks sales assistant at hardware store if he has any Plutonium in stock
9. Is bitterly disappointed to discover that current Miss Universe is from Earth

10. Orders policemen to 'take me to your leader' before being deported on charges of being an illegal alien

TOP TEN POLITICIANS WHOSE NAMES HAVE BECOME VERBS

1. Allan Boesak. To 'Boesak' is to thunderingly proclaim one's innocence in the face of mounting evidence to the contrary. As in: 'I cannot tell a lie. Someone else cut down the cherry tree,' Boesakked George Washington, hiding the axe behind his back and trying to make himself understood through a mouthful of cherry pips

2. Mangosuthu Gatsha Buthelezi. To 'Gatsha' is to force one's way into a cosy private gathering, as in 'Just as the Hendersons were sitting down to enjoy the first course of their Golden Anniversary dinner, an off-course parachutist Gatshaed through the roof of their Sandton mansion

3. Jay Naidoo. To 'Naidoo' is to resort to beguiling obfuscation in the cause of seeking greater transparency, as in 'Don't Naidoo me!' she yelled, as her husband attempted to explain that the lipstick on his collar was a speck of tomato sauce left over from a lunchtime board meeting on

aspects of implementing the Reconstruction and Development Programme

4. Ferdi Hartzenberg. To 'Hartzenberg' is to mysteriously disappear from the scene, as in 'I parked my car in a secure bay at Sandton City, and when I returned from shopping only nine hours later, I was shocked to discover that it had Hartzenberged,' she informed her insurance broker on the cellphone

5. Pik Botha. To 'Pik' is to commit a glaring indiscretion at a social gathering, as in 'Will you be having a single or a double Jack Daniels?' he asked, Pikking up an empty glass and pointing it in the direction of the Iranian Minister for Energy Affairs

6. Eugene Terre'Blanche. To 'Terre'Blanche' is to attempt to recover one's decorum after momentarily misplacing it in public, as in 'Rising slowly from the bottom of the marsh, the General re-mounted his stallion and Terre'Blanched valiantly into the field of battle'

7. Winnie Mandela. To 'Winnie' is to emerge unscathed and triumphant

from a blistering attack on one's personal integrity. As in: 'Hooray! I'm free!' Winnied the company director, striding out of Pretoria Central after serving three minutes of a 20-year sentence for pension fund fraud

8. Patricia de Lille. To 'Delille' is to draw attention to oneself through shrill proclamation, as in 'It's absolute rubbish to suggest that the PAC wants to drive all whites into the sea,' she Delilled. 'We'd far rather they got out and walked'

9. Tony Leon. To 'Tonyleon' is to harangue through constant whining, as in 'Just as I was about to fall asleep in front of the television, a mosquito flew in through the window and Tonyleoned me on the back of my neck'

10. Roelf Meyer. To 'Roelf' is to go out of one's way to strike a compromise between diametrically opposing forces, as in 'Faced with a choice of fish or steak for the main course, he Roelfed in agony for several minutes before deciding to order the chicken'

TOP TEN PARLIAMENTARY COMMITTEES CURRENTLY IN SESSION

1. Committee to Investigate Why Jay Naidoo Hasn't Received His Cabinet Portfolio Yet
2. Committee to Investigate Ways of Persuading the Iranians to Buy Mossgas
3. Committee to Investigate Whether Members of the Parliamentary Press Corps Should Be Allowed To Stand In For Absentee Parliamentarians During Post Office Budget Vote
4. Committee to Investigate Whether Exterior of Parliament Should Be Redecorated In Traditional Ndebele Style
5. Committee to Allocate Additional Parking Bays For Ronnie Kasrils' Corvettes
6. Committee to Investigate Whether Consent Should Be Granted For Parliament To Be Used As Regular Venue For 'Raves'
7. Committee to Investigate Morality of Selling Arms to China, Cuba, Iran, Nicaragua, And Other

Countries With Appalling Credit Records

8. Committee to Implement Emergency Drills to Avoid Rush On Exits When Minister of Home Affairs Rises to Deliver His Budget Vote

9. Committee to Investigate Why You Can Never Find A Salt Cellar That Works In The Parliamentary Canteen

10. Committee to Investigate Why No One Has Turned Up For The Committee Meeting

Warning: this bay reserved for Ronnie Kasrils' Corvette

TOP TEN SUGGESTIONS FOR A NEW NAME FOR THE FREE STATE

1. The Orange Free State
2. The Interest Free State
3. The Lost Province
4. Gateway to the Sea
5. Marobalong (Place of Sleeping)
6. OranGauteng
7. Kwa-Vrystaat
8. Truckers' Rest
9. Flatlandia
10. Utopia

Formerly known as Free State

TOP TEN MOST VALUABLE ITEMS REPORTED 'MISSING' FROM SABC HEADQUARTERS

1. Extremely rare wall-size oil painting of Groot Marico landscape by Pierneef, last seen as studio backdrop during Agenda interview with Prince Sifiso Zulu
2. 'Beginner's Guide to BetaCam Operation', urgently required by CCV's Outside Broadcast Unit
3. John Bishop's moustache
4. Felicia Mabuza-Suttle's left shoulder-pad, last seen being kicked into touch by Joel Stransky during the World Cup rugy final
5. Very Old Stinkwood Round-Table, urgently required for round-table debates on Agenda-Newsline
6. Viewer, urgently required for round-table debates on Agenda-Newsline
7. Dr Ivy Matsepe-Casaburri, last seen correcting spelling of name on internal memorandums
8. Freek Robinson's navy-blue suit-jacket, last seen flying out of

seventh-floor window under power of its own lapels

9. Approximately two-and-a-half-million cash-slips required as proof of 'Subsistence and Transport' claims filed by SABC producers on outside assignment

10. 'Official Pronunciation Guide For SAfm Broadcasters', urgently required to prevent any of them from slipping into Standard English

The mystery of the SABC's missing Pierneef masterpiece solved at last

TOP TEN NEW UNDERGRADUATE COURSES AT WITS UNIVERSITY

1. Post-Modern Deconstructivism in Neo-Classical Architecture: How to hurl an over-full rubbish-bin through the windows of Senate House
2. Principles of Indoor Hydroelectric Re-Engineering: What happens when you turn on all the fire-hoses and short-circuit the mains box in the corridors of the Administration Building
3. New Approaches to Political Science: Boycotting science lectures on the grounds that they're not political enough
4. Accelerated Learning Programme: A hands-on approach to hijacking an administrator's car and driving it at high speed into the library foyer
5. Principles and Techniques of Mass Media Communication: Practical approaches to on-camera toyi-toyiing and breakfast television debates with the university authorities
6. Fundamentals of Applied Quantum Mechanics: How much sugar you

need to put in the tank of an administrator's car before the engine seizes up completely

7. Higher Education Through Advanced Computer Programming (1): The art and science of gaining remote terminal access to midyear examination papers on the university's mainframe computer

An undergraduate student preparing to undergraduate at a major South African tertiary institution

8. Higher Education Through Advanced Computer Programming (2): Watching what happens when two or more personal computers are dropped simultaneously from the second floor of the Computer Science Department
9. Basic Environmental Impact Assessment: Tabulating the immediate and long-term effects of 25 000 students toyi-toyiing on the flower beds around Senate House
10. Understanding Chaos Theory: How to get a university degree without actually attending lectures or writing exams

TELKOM'S TOP TEN FUN THINGS YOU CAN DO WITH YOUR TELEPHONE

1. Call Larry King Live on CNN – he loves hearing opinions from faraway places!

2. If you've got teenage kids, install extra phone-lines – it'll keep them out of your hair for hours at a time!

3. Any complaints, problems, or queries, call our special consumer 'Hold-On' line – enjoy full-length classical music symphonies while you wait!

4. Want to keep in touch with political developments in KwaZulu-Natal? Call Mangosuthu Buthelezi's exclusive 'Speech-Line' – you'll never want to say goodbye!

5. Play the 'Cellphone Game' – dial 082 followed by any seven digits, and see if you can guess where the person is when you reach them!

6. Ever get the feeling that you're a little behind the times? Dial 1026 and stay tuned – you'll have the time of your life!

7. Somewhere out there on the wild blue ocean, a ship at sea is waiting for your call!

8. Not sure how many noughts in a million? Simply enter our monthly 'Million Buck Lucky Telephone Subscriber Draw', and we'll send you the bill!

9. Ever wanted to be famous throughout the world? Just pick up the phone, call someone you love, and see if you can chat for long enough to earn a place in the Guinness Book of Records!

10. Play a fun practical joke on your friend or co-worker – wait till they go away for a few weeks, hook their phone-line to the Internet, and watch their faces when they get the bill!

PAC'S TOP TEN SLOGANS FOR THE 1999 GENERAL ELECTION

1. You've Tried Peace, Harmony, and Reconciliation – Now Give Us A Chance
2. When it Comes to Strong, Charismatic Leadership, Nothing Beats the PAC
3. Arms for the Poor
4. Vote X For President
5. Tomorrow Is Another Country – Azania
6. Vote PAC, and You'll Never Need to Vote For Another Party Again
7. One Settler, Too Many
8. This Time, Remember, It's The Congress With 'Africanist' In the Middle
9. Election? Didn't We Already Have An Election?
10. Tonight We're Going to Party Like It's 1999

THE SABC'S TOP TEN REASONS WHY YOU SHOULD PAY YOUR TELEVISION LICENCE

1. You will be able to go to sleep with a clear conscience while watching Good Morning South Africa
2. Part of your fee will go towards a haircut and a new set of jacket elbow patches for Max du Preez
3. Martin Bailie has applied to join the SABC's team of house-to-house television licence inspectors
4. Only registered licence-holders are entitled to enter the SABC's fabulous new 'Win A Free Television Licence' competition
5. Your timely contribution will help ease the SABC's huge burden of retrenchment payouts to personnel who would otherwise have to be sacked
6. Police File will soon feature a special section for television licence defaulters
7. If found guilty of watching television without a licence, you could be detained for up to three months in a prison cell with only a television set for company

8. Why spend several Rand a day hiring videos, when the same amount of money entitles you to the full range of SABC programming on all three channels?
9. On second thoughts, don't answer that
10. Pay your licence by the end of the year, and you could stand in line for one of several exclusive appointments to the SABC Board

What happens to people who fail to pay their SABC television licence

TOP TEN THINGS TO DO ON A SATURDAY NIGHT IN ORANIA

1. Patrol perimeter fence to make sure Nelson Mandela did not set a precedent
2. Tune in to TV1 at 8pm, to see whether Government has declared an independent Afrikaner Volkstaat yet
3. Stick around for 'LA Law'
4. Wonder how much Arnie Becker would charge to fight Government in Constitutional Court
5. Put mag wheels on ox-wagon
6. Wonder if it's worth driving 350km to the nearest Chinese takeaway for a Chop Suey and a packet of Spring Rolls
7. Telephone householders at random to inform them that they have won a free timeshare holiday opportunity in Orania
8. Count sheep
9. Spend a pleasant hour or two in the community hall, listening to classic hits by Elvis Presley

10. Ask Elvis how long he plans to stay in town

The latest addition to the growing list of celebrities who have paid courtesy visits to Orania

AZANIAN STUDENT MOVEMENT'S TOP TEN EDUCATION CRISIS DEMANDS

1. Only black chalk to be used on blackboards from now on
2. No more White Papers on Education to be issued by Government
3. Those big white areas on maps of the world must go
4. Schools to supply Magic Markers in assortment of colours for use on protest placards
5. Appearances on Agenda-Newsline to count towards Matric Oral marks
6. Racist talkshow hosts to stop asking us if we're racists
7. Schools to close early every Wednesday for start of 'Mass Action Long Weekend'
8. All Eng. Lit. setbooks to be replaced by Ice-T records
9. No more trigonometry homework
10. Come to think of it, we're not that crazy about being taught by black teachers either

TOP TEN EXCUSES FOR ABSENTEE PARLIAMENTARIANS

1. Thought it was against Standing Orders to attend a sitting of Parliament

2. Phoned to say I wouldn't be able to make it, but Speaker's cellphone was constantly engaged

3. Already attended Parliament once this year

4. Booked off by doctor after dropping Annual Expense Account claim on my foot

5. Had to rush out to attend to urgent business in my constituency, only to discover that I don't actually have one

6. Was halfway to Parliament, when I suddenly realised I'd left my Walkman at home

7. Spilled gravy on my tie during breakfast in Parliamentary canteen, had to go shopping for a new one

8. Flew to Bloemfontein by mistake – thought Parliament had already moved

9. Sent urgent registered express letter explaining why I wouldn't be able to attend debate on Postal Services Bill

10. Budget Vote clashed with an extraordinary meeting of the Special Select Committee to investigate ways of improving working conditions for Members of Parliament

TOP TEN INCORRECT FORMS OF ADDRESS FOR FW DE KLERK

1. Mr Second Deputy President
2. Mr Secondary Deputy President
3. Mr Second-Hand Deputy President
4. Mr Alternative Deputy President
5. Mr Affirmative Deputy President
6. Mr Immediate Past President
7. Mr Lance Reserve Deputy Sub-President
8. Mr FW Deputy President
9. Mr President-In-Waiting
10. Mr Deputy Nobel Laureate

BANTU HOLOMISA'S TOP TEN STORAGE SITES FOR TOXIC WASTE

1. The Big Hole, Kimberley. If we don't fill it up soon, somebody could fall in and hurt themselves
2. The Zoo Lake, Johannesburg. It's the only way we're going to stop that proposed waterfront shopping centre development
3. Programme Archives Department, SABC. Nobody will ever notice the difference
4. Top of Table Mountain, Cape Town. Green cloud will make a nice change after all these years
5. Eugene Nyati's bank account. Biggest bottomless pit in the country
6. Cango Caves. Toxic waste's proven 'glow-in-the-dark' quality will save millions in underground lighting
7. Plettenberg Bay. Toxic waste has only half as much environmental impact as Gauteng holidaymakers
8. French Embassy, Pretoria. Special delivery from New Zealand Embassy, Pretoria

9. Koeberg Nuclear Plant, Cape Town. They don't produce nearly enough toxic waste of their own

10. Mossgas. Biggest toxic waste of taxpayers' money in South African history

One of South Africa's top ten storage sites for toxic waste

TOP TEN SIGNS THAT THE INDEPENDENT AIRLINE YOU'RE TRAVELLING ON IS ABOUT TO GO BUST

1. Pilot drops pay-cheque on way into cockpit, and it bounces right back up

2. Airplane takes off with wheels still clamped due to non-payment of overnight parking fee

3. Aviation fuel attendant insists on cash upfront before filling tanks

4. Stewardess neglects to say 'Hope to see you again soon' to disembarking passengers

5. Return ticket includes free tent and sleeping-bag for camping in departure lounge of foreign airport

6. First Class passengers told they have to pay for hot towels

7. During emergency drill, stewardess asks passengers if they would mind sharing flotation jackets in unlikely event of liquidation

8. In-flight magazine replaced by photostat copies of Sheriff's Order of Attachment

9. Co-pilot asks if there are any labour attorneys on board, would they please identify themselves to the cabin crew

10. Supper is choice between salted peanuts and after-dinner mint

The pilot of an independent South African airline attempts to pocket his pay-cheque

TOP TEN REASONS WHY YOU'RE NOT ALLOWED TO USE A CELLULAR PHONE IN A BANK

1. Sharp ringing tone might wake up lady at Enquiries
2. Cellular signals might interfere with automatic door-jamming mechanism
3. Spouse might call and instruct you to cancel mortgage agreement
4. Difficulty of conducting intelligent telephone conversation while wearing full-face motorcycle helmet
5. Possibility of confusion caused by pointing cellular phone at teller and answering gun
6. You might phone around and compare motor vehicle finance charges
7. Constant use of cellphone in bank could nullify your application for an overdraft to pay your cellular phone account
8. Several clients reaching for cellphone in pocket at same time could cause security guard to panic and reach for own cellphone

9. Possibility that you might call switchboard and ask to be put through to Foreign Exchange clerk after unsuccessfully attempting to make eye contact for the last 45 minutes

10. In event of emergency, you might confuse your cellphone and ATM PIN numbers

Why you should not wear a full-face helmet while using a cellular phone in a bank

The Satellite-Dish Braai –
a hot new South African lifestyle accessory

TOP TEN WAYS SATELLITE TELEVISION WILL CHANGE YOUR LIFE

1. You won't want to go to sleep with 16 channels beaming sport, news, music, movies, drama, cartoons, and documentaries from the furthest corners of the globe
2. You won't be able to go to sleep for the constant fear that someone is about to back a construction crane up to your garden wall and drive off with your satellite dish
3. You will have something other than the relative signal strengths of cellular telephone service providers to talk about at dinner parties
4. You won't have to go to dinner parties
5. By linking your infrared home alarm system to your satellite dish, you will be able to enjoy 24-hour satellite surveillance of your armed response company
6. By adjusting your satellite dish to reflect the sun's ultraviolet rays at their noonday peak, you will be able to enjoy a delicious braai

without going to all the trouble of getting the Weber out of the garage

7. You will gain valuable insights into the constellations of the southern hemisphere by rushing outside every few minutes to check whether the PAS-4 satellite has fallen out of the sky, and if not, why you haven't been able to get a halfway decent picture

8. You will be able to catch up on all the classic movies you missed on TV1 because you had already walked out of the bioscope when they were first on circuit 35 years ago

9. You will be able to monitor CNN 24 hours a day in the hope that Saddam Hussein will improve the quality of programming by invading Kuwait again

10. You will have to spend several hours in a private clinic having a giant callus removed from the thumb you use to operate the remote-control

TOP TEN REASONS WHY JOHANNESBURG IS A BETTER PLACE TO STAY THAN CAPE TOWN

1. No giant mountain to interfere with cellular phone reception
2. Plenty to read on cardboard signs while waiting for lights to change
3. Elegant historical buildings in city centre are routinely imploded to make way for glass skyscrapers
4. Plentiful transport to and from city – just wait at a stop street and ask the first driver who comes along to get out and give you the keys
5. No annoying seagulls to interfere with enjoyment of meal at waterfront shopping centres
6. Parking available right outside main entrances to shopping centres, as long as you get there before the disabled drivers do
7. People don't walk around all day with zinc sunblock on their noses
8. Better freeway system means up to 20 per cent quicker armed response times
9. Place isn't full of stressed-out

Gauteng advertising executives looking for beachside rental property to convert to a restaurant

10. No matter where you are, you're never more than two hours away from the nearest casino resort development

TOP TEN COMPLAINTS FILED AGAINST SOUTH AFRICAN COMPETITORS BY EGYPTIAN DELEGATION TO ALL-AFRICA GAMES

1. SA netball team not chosen on merit – some members were white
2. Too many colours in SA flag
3. 'Shosholoza' is rude word in Arabic
4. SA pole-vault champion was assisted by a Pole
5. SA competitor in hammer-throw event deliberately cracked knuckles while waiting for Egyptian competitor to finish
6. SA swimmers made loud gulping noises during Butterfly event
7. SA gold medal-winners have conflict of interests because medals are made from SA gold
8. SA hurdles champion is an imposter – doesn't look anything like his passport-photo
9. SA javelin-thrower slapped javelin against rawhide shield before throwing
10. Several Egyptian competitors suffered from food poisoning as result of eating sour grapes

TOP TEN WAYS TO MAKE A MILLION BUCKS WITHOUT REALLY TRYING

1. Submit invoice for R100 to Provincial Premier's Office, and add four noughts by mistake
2. Accept appointment as Chief Executive of small independent bank, and approve interest-free loan to Chief Executive of small independent bank
3. Accept scaled-down fee for consulting to Government on ways of scaling-down fees for Government consultants
4. Form Non-Government Organisation (NGO), and apply to Danish Government for funding to cover Allan Boesak's legal expenses
5. Obtain rare R200 note, and photocopy 5 000 times to prove ownership in event of theft
6. Dig hole in garden, fill with water, and sell to consortium of waterfront shopping centre developers
7. Stencil 'Whites Only' on rusty squares of sheet metal, and sell to

American tourists as authentic relics of apartheid era

8. Offer to act as go-between in wage negotiations between Louis Luyt and Springbok rugby squad

9. Spend two million bucks on Ithuba Win 'n Spin tickets

10. Make withdrawal from pot of gold at end of rainbow

How to make a million bucks, the hard way

TOP TEN MOST COMMON CAUSES OF 'FALSE ALARMS' REPORTED TO ARMED RESPONSE COMPANIES

1. Inadvertent use of panic button to change channel during supermarket ad featuring Martin Bailie
2. Incorrect alarm-deactivation code keyed in after cash-card mysteriously swallowed by ATM at bank
3. Cat leaping in path of infrared intruder-detection beam in bid to avoid intruder crawling along floor
4. Half-brick thrown through kitchen window by departing householder attempting to retrieve car-keys from table with stick
5. Home alarm system spontaneously activated in response to incessantly wailing car alarm across the road
6. Householder pausing to answer cellular phone in 30-second 'grace period' between opening of front door and deactivation of alarm
7. Unsuccessful attempt to steal household alarm system by burglar planning to return later to steal household contents

8. Short-circuit caused by householder striking wiring of alarm system while drilling hole to accommodate list of emergency numbers

9. Alarm automatically activated by householder's scream at learning of insurance company's refusal to pay out for prior robbery on account of faulty alarm system

10. One-year guarantee on alarm system just expired

One of the most common causes of false alarms reported to armed response companies

TOP TEN USES FOR A FORCIBLY REMOVED STATUE OF HF VERWOERD

1. Melt down and turn into millions of tiny one-cent pieces, to be used when paying speeding-fines in Orania
2. Enjoy 12,5 per cent discount on household insurance premiums by placing on lawn as burglar deterrent
3. Store safely under lock and key on Robben Island for 27 years
4. Offer to Johannesburg Zoo as attractive centrepiece for pigeon aviary
5. Offer to SABC as dynamic new presenter for Good Morning South Africa
6. Install in cinema foyer as part of advance promotional display for 'Return to Jurassic Park: the Sequel'
7. Offer to AWB to use as hostage during negotiations for independent Afrikaner Volkstaat
8. Place against door of Agenda studio to prevent Minister of Home Affairs from gaining unauthorised entry

9. Smash into thousands of little pieces, and sell at fleamarkets to help fund Reconstruction and Development Programme
10. Decorate with garish splashes of day-glo paint, turn upside-down, and sell to Everard Read Art Gallery for R750 000

What to do with a forcibly removed statue of an architect of apartheid

TOP TEN DEMOCRATIC PARTY CAMPAIGN PROMISES FOR 1999

1. No South African will be denied the right to housing, education, healthcare, employment, and a decent breakfast television service
2. Vote DP now, and we promise we won't bother you for the rest of the Millennium
3. We've got a plan to keep criminals off the streets
4. And we're working on a plan to keep them out of our houses
5. Give us your mandate, and we'll fight tooth and nail for an increase in the quota of English on SAfm
6. No import duty on handmade Italian leather loafers
7. Four-day working week for domestic workers, with negotiable increase in minimum wage to make up for extra day
8. More cellphone base stations in hilly areas of Gauteng
9. If you think the ANC has no idea how to govern the country, just give us a chance

10. We promise to continue and expand our comprehensive feeding scheme for the squirrels in Parliament Gardens

The Democratic Party launches its comprehensive new feeding scheme for Parliamentary squirrels

Pizza-on-Rollerblades Delivery Trainee – a white male graduate enters the South African job market

TOP TEN EMPLOYMENT OPPORTUNITIES FOR WHITE MALE GRADUATES

1. Classified Advertisement Proofreader
2. Foreign Consulate Interior Decor Consultant
3. Assistant Truth and Reconciliation Commission Lie-Detector Operator
4. Freelance Pizza-on-Rollerblades Delivery Trainee
5. Springbok Rugby Captain
6. Endangered Wildlife Trust Fundraiser
7. Senior Executive, National Sorghum Breweries
8. Product tester for new range of Zero Protection Factor suntan lotions
9. Speech Input Typist for Minister of Home Affairs
10. White Male Postgraduate

GREG BLANK'S TOP TEN COMPLAINTS ABOUT PRISON LIFE

1. Unrestricted use of cellphones interferes with satellite television reception
2. Warders routinely beat prisoners at ping-pong
3. Laundry just doesn't seem to be able to get these stubborn stains out of my white collar
4. Sick and tired of journalists telling me I look like Tim Robbins in 'The Shawshank Redemption'
5. Too much salt in the gazpacho last night
6. Stockbrokers just want to talk shop all day
7. Nothing higher than Factor 10 sunblock available in the exercise yard
8. Not enough bars in this place – just try getting a decent Martini after 10pm
9. Hardly anything to read in here but Time and Life
10. Constantly worry that I might be let out early for good behaviour

No Factor 11 Sunblock available in exercise yard – one of Greg Blank's top ten complaints about prison life in South Africa

MANGOSUTHU BUTHELEZI'S TOP TEN PUBLIC SPEAKING TIPS

1. For dramatic impact, pause for breath every 3 000 words or 45 seconds, whichever comes first
2. To overcome severe attack of stage fright, ask frightened person to leave stage before you begin speaking
3. Two best ways to silence hecklers: urgent Supreme Court interdict, or rolled-up copy of speech
4. Before banging fist on podium to emphasise point, make sure that jug of iced water has been safely removed
5. Be alert for signs of fidgeting, hacking, and general discomfort among your audience – it could mean that there is a problem with the air-conditioning
6. Reward audiences for their patience by announcing, as you reach end of four-and-a-half-hour speech, that you will now repeat the whole thing in Zulu
7. If you find yourself suffering from insomnia on the eve of a big public

speaking engagement, spend a few minutes reciting speech to yourself in mirror

8. Avoid jokes about sex, politics, and religion, unless you can link them directly to the ANC's draft proposals for a Bill of Rights

One of the major causes of stage fright – being on the same stage as Home Affairs Minister Mangosuthu Buthelezi

9. Cut down on long, rambling, incomprehensible speeches by bursting on to the stage and grabbing the microphone for yourself

10. When using overhead projectors to illustrate speech, insert the first few slides upside-down to check whether audience is paying attention

TOP TEN NEW SERVICES OFFERED BY THE POST OFFICE

1. Super Priority Deluxe Express: Mail upgraded to special super-fast computerised sorting queue for urgent attention of person coming to fix computer in two weeks' time
2. Guaranteed Same-Day Immediate Transit: Mail is stamped, franked, scanned, bar-coded, signed, sealed, sorted and lost within minutes of being handed in at any Post Office across the country
3. Special Overnight Urgent Delivery: Mail containing valuables, postal orders, and confidential documents is entrusted to elite team of specially trained motorcycle couriers for guaranteed delivery to their home addresses
4. Registered Overseas Confirmed Parcel-Post Priority: Free personalised follow-up service to confirm that parcels sent to overseas destinations have unfortunately failed to arrive due to mix-up on other side
5. Rapid Post-Haste Insured Parcel Notification Service: Persons to

whom bulky insured parcels are addressed are telephonically informed that some brown paper and a couple of pieces of string are awaiting collection at the Post Office, and would the person who sent the goods kindly claim from insurance

Revealed at last: why you never got that cheque that was in the post

6. Rapid Remuneration Red-Letter Priority Express: Your cheque is in the post
7. Inter-Urban Express Delivery Re-Routing Service: Guaranteed hand delivery of your mail as soon as police are able to track down person who hijacked postman's bicycle
8. Personal Wealth Creator Investment Maximisation Opportunity: Buy Ithuba ticket at counter
9. Centralised Neighbourhood Priority Mail Pick-Up Progamme: Residents without Post Boxes may collect mail at their own convenience from bottom of stormwater drain
10. Guaranteed Double-Your-Money-Back Nationwide Express Delivery Initiative: For small surcharge, friendly Post Office personnel will supply sender with address and telephone number of nearest 'PostNet' franchise

TOP TEN MONEY-MAKING TIPS FOR GOVERNMENT COST-CUTTING CONSULTANTS

1. Remember, there are only 24 hours in a day – so consider charging by the minute
2. Make life easier for your accountants by rounding off expense claims to the nearest R10 000
3. Put aside a few hundred thousand Rand in a high interest-bearing call account, in case you have to pay it all back when you've finished consulting
4. Advise Government to cut costs by retrenching independent auditors
5. Reduce personal tax burden by insisting on being paid in cash
6. Take care of the 1s, and the 0s will take care of themselves
7. Be sure to carry an extra large briefcase to work every morning, especially if you're consulting at the Mint
8. Lunch, golf, and cocktail receptions are intrusions on your

valuable working schedule, so be sure to charge double

9. Always fly Economy instead of First Class on official business, and don't forget to pocket the difference

10. Remember the secret formula of success: 99 per cent consultation, and one per cent perspiration

TOP TEN PHOTO OPPORTUNITIES FOR PRESIDENT NELSON MANDELA

1. Organise 'forgive and forget' tea-party for Presidential spouse in gardens of Union Buildings
2. Go horse-riding with Eugene Terre'Blanche, albeit not on same horse
3. Accept guest role as 'Mister President' in new series of Egoli
4. Launch stunning new range of 'invisible ties' at gala fashion banquet
5. Throw first dice at official opening of Robben Island Waterworld and Casino
6. Go three rounds with Mike Tyson on eve of heavyweight contest at Sun City
7. Host weekly chat show, 'Long Talk to Freedom', on Radio 702
8. Wait until SABC cameraman falls backwards into fishpond while filming walkabout with foreign Head of State, and rush forward to make sure fish are all right

9. Donate Springbok rugby cap and jersey to Claremont branch of ANC, to assist in paying off outstanding cellular phone bills

10. Make unannounced election campaign call on neighbour in Houghton, and spend next few hours posing for photographs with Armed Response patrol officers